A World Full of Wonderful Things

Written by Amber Lily

Illustrated by James Newman Gray

IMAGINE THAT

Licensed exclusively to Imagine That Publishing Ltd
Tide Mill Way, Woodbridge, Suffolk, IP12 1AP, UK
www.imaginethat.com
Copyright © 2021 Imagine That Group Ltd
All rights reserved
0 2 4 6 8 9 7 5 3 1
Manufactured in China

Written by Amber Lily
Illustrated by James Newman Gray

ISBN 978-1-80105-186-6

A catalogue record for this book is available from the British Library

The world is so full of wonderful things,
Take time to love what each day brings.

Drinking lemonade on a sunny day,

Meeting friends in the
park to joke and play.

Swimming in the bright, blue shimmering sea,
Splish, splash, splosh – happy as can be.

Toasting marshmallows on an open fire,

Singing with friends in a merry choir.

Ice skating on a cold, crisp winter's day,

Running and jumping through summer hay.

Biking around your
neighbourhood,

Helping others, so they feel good.

Hiking up a hill in the countryside,
Admiring the view from far and wide.

Dancing to music, tapping your feet,
A smile on your face, as you move to the beat.

Gazing up at the twinkling stars,
Looking out for the Moon and Mars.

Being brave and trying something new,
Mum and Dad are so proud of you!

Cuddling Mum and Dad
when you go to bed ...

Now it's time to rest your sleepy head.